PUFFIN BOOKS

SPACENAPPED!

'He pressed his hands
against the glass.
Five fingers on each hand …
I wondered if the extra finger
got in the way.'

Crowds are flocking to see the
new space creature. Not only is it
twice the size of a normal person
but it has only two eyes! But Tal is
suspicious. Is this thing trying to
communicate? And what are
those strange drops of moisture
coming out of its eyes? Soon Tal
is asking questions and the
answers are not what he'd like
them to be …

By the Same Author
Iggy From Outer Space
Dead Meat!
Dead Average!
Dead Worried!
Sit Down, Mum, There's Something I've Got to Tell You
Fourteen Something

MOYA SIMONS

SPACENAPPED!

ILLUSTRATED BY LEIGH HOBBS

PUFFIN BOOKS

Puffin Books
Penguin Books Australia Ltd
487 Maroondah Highway, PO Box 257
Ringwood, Victoria 3134, Australia
Penguin Books Ltd
Harmondsworth, Middlesex, England
Viking Penguin, A Division of Penguin Books USA Inc.
375 Hudson Street, New York, New York 10014, USA
Penguin Books Canada Limited
10 Alcorn Avenue, Toronto, Ontario, Canada M4V 3B2
Penguin Books (N.Z.) Ltd
182–190 Wairau Road, Auckland 10, New Zealand

First published by Penguin Books, 1996

1 3 5 7 9 10 8 6 4 2

Typeset in 10.5/16 Stone Serif
Made and printed in Australia by Australian Print Group, Maryborough,
Victoria

National Library of Australia
Cataloguing-in-Publication data:

Simons, Moya, 1942-.
Spacenapped!

ISBN 0 14 038192 9

I. Title.
A823.3

FOR LONI & YORAM
WITH LOVE

CHAPTER

1

Tal daydreams. He spends most of the day with a scroll crayon in his mouth gazing out the window at beeny hoppers and jetmobiles. Has brains but needs to keep all his eyes on his work.

Mum stared at my school report and made a low clicking sound.

'Just concentrate on the good news,' I told her. 'The part that says I've got brains.'

Mum flicked back her wriggly green curls, and all four of her eyes curled into a major frown. Her head always looks much bluer and pointier when she's angry.

'Don't give me that rubbish. You just don't work, Tal. You're twelve hecta-years old now. It's time you began to concentrate on your studies.' A small stress lump appeared on her forehead. 'Your father will be extremely disappointed.'

Oh no, I could practically see the lump growing. I'd completely freaked her out. Now she'd moan and click and carry on for hours.

'Do your homework, now!' she snapped. Soon my dad would come home. He'd get a stress lump the size of a dorpo when he saw my report scroll. He turns a horrible dark blue when he's really mad.

Dad's a zoologist with the Space Academy on Zordeth. He gets to visit all these zillygopping places collecting specimens for the Intergalactic Zoo. Mum teaches art at the University and gets to visit galleries and artists all over the galaxy. I get to hang around here and do my homework.

Oh well, that's life! A few of Mum's krystalumps might ease the pain. Maybe then I'd have the energy to do my homework.

I sneaked around the kitchen. Mum always hides the krystalumps just before I get home from school. They were probably behind the glass sun-stove – one of her favourite secret places. Ha ha. Or so she thought.

Both Mum and Dad love to cook, but Mum bakes the best krystalumps in the galaxy. She has her own secret recipe for the mineral mix, and she always rolls them in fresh carbon.

I'm not into cooking, I'm just into eating. At that moment my stomachs were so empty I was scared I'd stunt my growth if I didn't get some food right away.

'And don't you dare start on the krystalumps, you'll spoil your appetite for dinner. Just get on with your homework, do you hear me?'

'Yes, Mum. Sure thing, Mum. Whatever you say, Mum.' It's those extra ears in her feet. They pick up everything.

I went into my bedroom. Jetmobiles streaked across the clear pink sky. Just one more lesson and I'd be up there with the best of them. Zinging across Zordeth, zonging off to nearby planets. I could visit my scroll friend Diti on her planet and maybe we could go skimskating down a few volcanoes.

I sat at my desk and watched its rainbow colours swirling everywhere. They're supposed to help me concentrate. Under the desk was a glob of yesterday's gubblebum. I put it in my mouth and took out my scroll pen and pad. I had to write a dumb story for my dumb teacher.

'Complete this sentence: "One day when I was coming home from school ... " then write a story about some gigglegopping thing that happened before you reached home.'

'Tal. Come here. Now.'

Oh, no. It was Dad. I could hear him beeping and squeaking to Mum. I bet his forehead was already growing a stress lump.

I got up slowly, like that eight-legged octofruntus at the Zoo. I mean, who'd rush to their own execution?

Dad was in the cushy-cove room, swinging in his cushy cove. Soft lava bubbles massaged his back, but he didn't look very relaxed. His face was deep blue, his eyes were twisted into a threatening scowl, and he was punching himself to show how totally furious he was.

'Hi, Dad,' I said brightly, curling my eyes into my best, most appealing smile.

'Don't try that on me, Tal. I've just read your report scroll and I'm totally furious. Great bells of banglee, you'll never be a space zoologist if you get marks like these.'

'Maybe I'm not cut out to be a space zoologist, Dad. Maybe ...'

Dad punched himself again.

'You'll end up grinding rocks for flour if you

don't start concentrating on your studies. Unless your results improve there'll be no more jetmobile lessons.'

'But Dad, that's not fair. I'm almost qualified. You can't do that to me.'

'I can and I have and that's that. Either your marks pick up or I'll tell your instructor your final lesson is cancelled.'

'But San says I'm the best pupil he's ever had. He reckons I'm one of a kind.'

Two of my father's eyes peered at me while the others rolled around in his head. 'That's true. You're definitely one of a kind. Now go back to your room and don't come down until dinner is ready. Get stuck into your school work. Great folly-foops. As if I don't have enough to worry about. The Space Academy's cutting back on staff ... I could lose my job! Now get back to your room and do your homework.'

'Yes, Dad,' I said as I backed out of the room.

Dad lose his job? Impossible. After all, he was the guy who'd brought back the Fingals from Phonia – those silver spiders with the huge green eyes. And what about the two-headed creature from the end of the galaxy? One of the heads bit my dad on his little blue arm and he still had the teeth marks.

That must count for something. Fire my dad? Leaping lollyfrogs! Never.

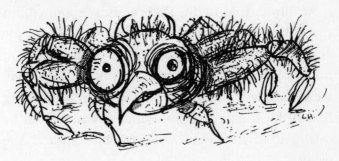

Over the next few days I worked hard at school. I didn't have any choice. Mum's eyes were continually curled into miserable frowns whenever she talked to me. Dad just stared at me and clicked in disappointment. So I did my best. At the end of the week I wrote a note to my parents in my best scroll writing.

I am happy to tell you that your son, Tal, has applied himself diligently to his work this week and is now doing very well. I have great hopes for him.

Then I signed the teacher's name. There! That showed true consideration for my parents. After all, I didn't want my father stressing out about my school work when he could lose his job.

Mum and Dad were very pleased with my kind

note. Dad even jumped on my feet to show how happy he was. 'Good on you, Tal,' he said.

At dinner that night, Dad carefully spooned out the grilled rock. Mum broke off a piece of soot pie and said, 'You know, Tal, you're going to be on holiday soon. Since your school work has improved, we've decided you can go on with your final flying lesson. By the end of the holidays you should be qualified to fly your own jetmobile around the galaxy.'

I curved my eyes into appreciative smiles. This was very good. Even Dad smiled.

'Just keep up the wonderful school reports,' he said.

'I will,' I replied, already planning my next scroll note. 'But Dad, what's happening at the Space Academy?'

Dad stroked his skinny chin. 'It's like this, Tal. We're short of money. The government isn't prepared to fund too many space trips, which means we can't collect enough specimens for the Zoo. But we've just finished making an amazing new spaceship. We can achieve gigadrive! We can go to parts of the universe we've never visited before. You remember me telling you about those radio beeps coming from the furthest corner of the universe?'

'Yes. You told me that we'd never find out if they were coming from intelligent beings because it would take too long to get there.'

Dad patted one of his stomachs. 'Quite so. Well, our new ship can get us there in hecta-secs. I won't explain the technology to you, but it's very simple to operate. Just one pull of a lever when you reach the far limits of our galaxy and – cabolla – cabang – you're there. Then it should be a simple matter of following the source of the radio beeps. And if those beeps mean that there's life out there, there are probably lots of exotic creatures. If the Intergalactic Zoo can attract crowds again, then our financial problems will be over and there won't be staff cutbacks.'

Dad reached for some more grilled rock.

'But what if you find intelligent beings? That'd be terrific. Maybe I could find a new scroll friend to write to. Maybe … '

'Slow down, Tal,' said Dad. 'If they're intelligent beings the rule is I can't take them for the Zoo. Maybe we can learn something from their culture, but that's up to other scientists.

'It's the Zoo I'm worried about. I must find some new attraction. The crowds are dwindling and my job may be at stake.'

'Dad, if I work really, really hard at school, can't I come with you? I could help you. I could … '

'Forget it, Tal. I've got enough problems.' Dad waved his arm around then punched himself. 'The spaceship's only big enough for me and maybe one or two small specimens.'

'I'm sure you'll find something new, Veth darling,' said Mum cheerfully. 'After all, who brought back the Fingals from Phonia and the two-headed monsters from Exenia?'

'True,' said Dad, and he patted his nose with pride. 'Still, I've got to come up with something new. Tomorrow is an important day. I find out from the Academy if I can make the trip.'

CHAPTER

The next day Dad left early. He jumped affection-
ately on Mum's feet and then on mine.

'Bye, Veth,' said Mum, then turned to me. 'Off to
school, and remember, I only want to hear good
things about your work.'

I threw my scroll bag over my shoulder and
straightened my school hat. 'Sure thing, Mum,' I
said, pulling faces at a few of her space flowers
when she wasn't looking. I set off for school, but as
soon as I was out of sight I took off my hat and put
it in my pocket to make friends with my gubblebum, rock chocks and the zillion other bits and
pieces I needed to get by in life.

It was warm on the road, but then it's always that
way on Zordethian roads. Ever since that famous
inventor Otototo ran lava under our streets, travelling's very warm and cosy. Which is just as well

because Zordeth is a cold planet. We're so far from our sun that it's just a small orange dot in the sky.

School was at the end of my street – very handy. I could leave my house at the last minute and after school I was home in whiz-bang time. The building was super modern, with pointed glass tops, boulder walls and big triangular windows.

The schoolyard was covered in purple grass, and surrounded by tall trees with excellent branches. If they were in a good mood they didn't mind if you swung from a branch or two. I ran to catch up with my friend, Gike.

'Are you going away for the holidays?' he asked.

My eyes drooped. 'Not this year. Dad may be whizzing into space and Mum just wants to stay home. But at least I can finish my flying lessons. Did you know I'm getting a jetmobile for my birthday?'

'Fantastic! My parents want me to wait, but we can still go out in yours. We'll have a willyhopping time.'

We filed into the classroom with the other kids and sat down at our desks. They had the same swirling rainbow patterns as my desk at home. The patterns were meant to stimulate thinking, but the only thing they stimulated in me was an urge to jump out the window and find something better to do.

'Today, class, we are going to discuss Zordethian history. We are going to blah, blah, blah.'

I tried to keep all my eyes open, I really did, but the top ones slowly closed. I felt the others begin to droop. Maybe I didn't get enough sleep at night. Maybe ...

'Tal Xofloat!' I jumped. Ms Tibz was pointing at me with her glass ruler. 'You're a disgrace,' she snapped. 'Stand at the back of the room. You can hop and clap hands for the remainder of the lesson. Maybe that will keep you awake.'

And that's what I did. Kids giggled and pointed at me – a totally off experience. It would be a while before I fell asleep in class again.

After school I couldn't wait to leave. I jumped on Gike's feet, yelled goodbye and took off, rushing down the street, bumping into people wheeling their little kids in bubble prams.

When I got home Mum was already back from work and standing in the front garden, smiling encouragingly at her space flowers. They were taller than her with these gross purple cup leaves. And Mum was singing to them. Her voice was awful but they were swaying happily and singing back. They had no taste at all.

Just as I strolled up the pathway the speakphone blasted. The space flowers immediately stopped swaying and their leaves drooped. They were so dopey it was pathetic.

'Oh no,' said Mum. 'The speakphone's scared them. Tal, sing to them. You know how sensitive they are. Please.'

So while Mum ran to answer the speakphone, I was stuck with those off flowers. And anyone, just anyone, could have walked past our house and seen me standing there singing.

I clicked in a low miserable voice. The flowers began to straighten, curling leaves began to unfold. This was very good for the flowers but definitely not good for my reputation.

'Ha ha, look at that geek singing to his space flowers. Ha ha.'

It was Feto, the class pain, walking past my house on his way home with his eyes curled into the biggest grins you've ever seen.

'Get a one-way ticket to the end of the galaxy,' I shouted.

Mum came rushing back to me. 'Tal, your father just phoned. He's so excited. He's leaving tomorrow on that whiz-bang new spaceship.' She stopped smiling and frowned. 'I don't know whether to be pleased for him or not. It's risky. We don't know what's out there.'

Mum gently patted the petals of the space flowers. 'Sorry,' she told them. 'I've got to go inside now. You wouldn't want to sing to them a little longer, Tal?'

'No way. Not for all the krystalumps in Zordeth.

Anyway, I've got homework to do.'

That's always the way to get round my parents!

When Dad came home he was very excited. He jumped on our feet with such affection he nearly burst our shoes.

'What an honour. Such an adventure. I hoped they'd choose me. After all, I helped design the new spaceship. But still, it's wonderful. Now, all I need to do is find something special for our Zoo.'

'And a scroll friend for me to write to, Dad?'

'Leave that to other scientists, Tal. My concern is the Intergalactic Zoo. We've got to attract bigger crowds. I must come up with something new.'

'You will, I'm sure you will, Veth,' said Mum.

The evening passed quickly. I could hear Dad preparing for his trip while I sat at my window and watched the two silver moons of Zordeth. The sky was dotted with stars, and the bright lights of jet-mobiles flashed past. There was so much up there – I couldn't wait to get my licence.

Next morning, after a full breakfast of stone crispies and waxed herbal leaves, Dad grabbed his bag. I wanted to go with him to the spaceport but he said I couldn't.

'Your school work comes first, Tal. Don't pull that face. Remember the holidays. Your mother will drive me to the spaceport and before you know it I'll be home. I cut through the time barrier when I go into gigadrive, remember. Time will pass at a different rate for me. In a few of your days I'll be back. If everything's okay, that is.'

A small stress lump appeared on my dad's forehead. He was really freaking out. He might be excited but he was nervous as well. I jumped lightly on his shoes.

'Don't worry, Dad. You'll find the most wonderful specimens. You'll be promoted. You'll be famous. I'll be famous because I'm your son. You'll ...'

'Now now, Tal, take it easy.'

'Do you have your stunner gun? What about Mum's krystalumps?'

'Everything's packed. Goodbye, Tal.'

Dad jumped on my feet and twisted my nose. So

there I was – off to another inspiring day at school while my dad did something really ordinary like flying Zordeth's one and only gigadrive spaceship to the other side of the universe.

CHAPTER

3

Dad had gone, school holidays had begun and I was bored. My best friend, Gike, had left to visit his cousin who lives on Phlotzo, our neighbouring planet. They have wonderful beaches with grey sand and purple seas, and because it's closer to the sun it's warmer than Zordeth – you can get around in just a pair of pearly shorts most of the time.

The radio beeper in the kitchen crackled and said, 'Veth calling beloved family. Kindly respond.'

When Dad was away he could call in on the space transceiver. On this trip he'd been so far away he couldn't get more than a tiny beep through, so I was as excited as a floddle on a cloudy day.

I yelled into the round speakdish. 'Hey, Dad, it's me. What happened? Where are you? When are you coming home?'

'Tal, everything's gone very well.' Dad's muffled

voice came through. 'Where's your mother?'

'I can hear her in the garden. She's singing to those gross flowers.'

'Run out and tell her I'll be at the spaceport at fifteen hecta-hours.'

'Dad, quick, tell me. Is there anything out there? Did you find some new creature?'

'It's been very productive. Now, I have to contact the Space Academy, so I'll see you later.'

Dad had gone. I wondered what he'd brought back. What did 'very productive' mean exactly? I ran out to the front garden where Mum was singing in her out-of-tune voice to those daggy space flowers.

'Mum!' She stopped singing and turned around. 'Dad's just phoned. He'll be at the spaceport at fifteen hecta-hours.'

Mum jumped happily on my feet. 'Thank goodness,' she said. 'Did he tell you about his trip?'

'No, but he said it was very productive.'

She tweaked my nose, making it even flatter. I hated Mum doing that. I was twelve hecta-years old and I'd have my jetmobile licence soon. It was time for all that mushy stuff to stop.

Later in the afternoon Mum and I drove out to the spaceport to meet Dad, Number One Zoologist in the whole of Zordeth. Lots of people were running around, all clicking and carrying on, and I saw members of the Space Academy. Most of them were okay but there was one guy I definitely didn't like: Fiz. He had four of the meanest eyes you'd ever

seen and I reckoned they'd crack if he tried to smile. He definitely didn't like kids. Once I heard him say, 'I never speak to any child under fifteen hecta-years because they're as stupid as pillies in a pod.'

I'd mastered four galactic languages before I was ten, and was working on my own transpeaker to simultaneously interpret other languages. Not bad for a stupid pilly in a pod, eh? It took me ages to put it together, but I'll make a squillion hooberoos with it one day.

We walked with members of the Space Academy out along the glidepath to the big red spacefield where a lot of spacecraft were lined up in neat rows.

'Veth's craft has just landed,' Fiz told my mother. 'It will be most interesting to see what he has brought back.' He scratched his ugly blue chin.

'I can't wait to see Veth.' Mum patted her green curls and got this soppy look in all her eyes.

We passed lots of jetmobiles and beeny hoppers on the way to the ship. Beeny hoppers were for little kids. I used to have one. They were for dashing about Zordeth. You couldn't get into space with them. I looked at all the little kids standing around their hoppers and shook my head. I couldn't imagine why I used to get excited over mine.

I could see Dad's spaceship. The side panel had opened and ... what on Zordeth was that coming down the air chute from the ship? Dad was following it. It was some sort of space creature, but what?

I ran ahead. Dad looked tired, and even from here I could see he had a stress lump on his forehead, but I guess that was understandable. After all, he'd been out there, to the other side of the universe. Mum ran with me. The space creature couldn't move until Dad unzapped it. It just stood there. Mum didn't seem the least interested. She ran straight up to Dad and jumped on his shoes.

I ignored all the mushy stuff and stood staring at the alien.

The first things I noticed were its eyes. It only had two, and they were blue! It was higgboggling amazing. The creature was standing upright on two legs with two eyes at the front of its head. What a combination! And it was so big! Taller even than Fiz, who was very tall. Its skin was an awful shade of pinky-brown and its head was round. Imagine. No sign of a point. And lots of brown hair, not just on top but on the sides and back of its head. But the most extraordinary thing was that it was wearing clothes.

The Academy members walked slowly around the space creature. Fiz reached out and prodded the animal with his fingers. I didn't like him doing that. Even if the creature was zapped it could still feel things.

'Veth,' a member of the Academy said. 'This is, without a doubt, an amazing specimen, but it's wearing protective garments of some sort. Though the're odd I suppose they must be clothes. Wouldn't that indicate some sort of intelligence? After all, if this creature wears clothing it would imply a knowledge of clothing manufacture. You know the rule. We simply can't have intelligent beings in our Zoo.'

The rim of my dad's hat failed to conceal a large stress lump. He must have had a rotten time on the other side of the universe. I couldn't wait to ask him about it.

'It is not intelligent. It is part of a sub-species on the planet I visited.'

Mum interrupted. 'My husband is totally exhausted. Please let him come home now to rest. He can present his findings to you later.'

Dad smiled at Mum. 'Yes, I am very tired. When I am rested I shall appear at the Space Academy and tell you everything. I'll show you the pictures I took of the other side of the universe. Believe me, there is a great deal to talk about.'

'I want to know more now,' said Fiz and there was a nasty click in his voice.

'No,' someone else said. 'We can wait. We shall arrange for our latest acquisition to be transported to the Intergalactic Zoo. Go home, Veth, and when you are less exhausted you can tell us all about your trip.'

I took one last look at the space creature, before it was taken away to the Zoo bubble van. Dad unzapped it, but snapped it into obedience so that it could be led to the van. It really was awfully ugly. And that strange look in its eyes. I guessed that was

the kind of look creatures had on the other side of
the universe.

Later that night, after dinner, Dad stretched out
in his cushy cove.

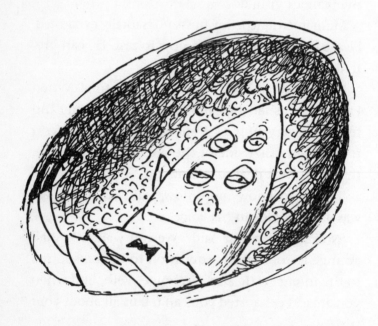

I'd been very patient. Mum had told me to wait
until Dad had eaten and rested before bombarding
him with questions. But great goggling grinobops I
couldn't wait any longer. It was all right for her –
I'd heard them talking for hours in their bedroom.

Now Mum was curled up in her workroom painting pictures of Zordethian sunsets or some other boring subject. She's crazy about painting. I crept into the cushy-cove room.

Dad was swinging in his cove. Volcanic bubbles made soft hissing noises and gently massaged his back.

'Dad,' I said, squatting on the glass floor beside him. 'Please tell me what it was like.'

Dad looked sad. 'It's very, very different from here, Tal. Going into gigadrive was exciting, and I had no trouble with the ship. But then I heard these awful noises – bangs and blasts like nothing I'd ever heard before. It was frightening. I followed these noises and eventually I came to a planetary system with one sun and nine planets. The noise coming out of the third planet was enough to give me a huge stress lump. Then I switched on my video screen to see if I could pick up anything. I was very excited, you can imagine.'

'Go on, Dad,' I said, because Dad was suddenly looking tired and two of his eyelids were starting to close.

'Well, some of the noise seemed to be coming from – and I know this is hard to believe – music. I saw strange creatures holding what must have been musical instruments, making the most appalling noise. You cannot imagine the number of notes they used. Zordeth's four magnificent notes make soft, soothing music. There, it sounded like a bizzle-bump having a bad day.'

Dad paused. He was looking very, very tired.

'I also saw great blue seas and buildings made of a strange substance and swarms of funny-looking creatures moving around. Some had arms and legs like us. Others had trunks and some had great humps on their back.'

'Did you say you saw buildings? Then the beings must be intelligent. But this creature – you said it wasn't intelligent.'

'Tal, I'm very tired, but I suppose I'd better explain. The creature I've brought back is a boy. Don't look so astonished, he's not a boy like you. He's a boy from the far side of the universe. I saw others of his species and he's definitely not full grown. Still, as you can see, he's very tall.'

'But … his clothing? And he had this look in his eyes. Almost like he was thinking.'

Three of Dad's eyes had closed. 'Tal,' he clicked quietly. 'He is a boy, that's true, and he wears clothing, that's true too. But he is part of a slave class on his planet. The clothing has been provided for him by the intelligent species. They have weapons and there are awful wars. I could have brought back some other alien, but many were too big, like the one with the huge, long trunk. Others were just not interesting enough. This boy will bring crowds back to the Zoo. Walking upright like us ... two legs like us ... two eyes. Fascinating, because I do believe he can see just as well with them as we can with four. Hmm ... zzzz.'

The fourth eye had closed. My dad was fast asleep while I was left with a squillion questions about life on the other side of the universe.

Oh well, never mind, I still had to make a few adjustments to my transpeaker, and some of Mum's krystalumps just might help me concentrate.

CHAPTER

4

It was two days later.

'Dad, please let me come to the Space Centre. I really want to hear your talk.'

Dad poured Mum some hot fiddlipod oil before he spoke.

Tal, I have to speak before a huge crowd of important people today. I've told you before – no children are allowed at the Space Centre.'

'But Dad – I could go with Mum. Please. I'll be so quiet no one will know I'm there.'

'There are no two ways about it, Tal. You just can't come. Look, tonight I'll show you the pictures I took of the boy's planet. I'll answer all your questions. You won't miss a thing.'

I left the table and went into the cushy-cove room. I was so cranky I gave myself two good hard punches. I climbed into the cove and tried to plan my day. I could work on my transpeaker, or then again I could visit the Zoo. That was it! I'd go and see the space boy. I'd make sure he was comfortable in his cage and that they were feeding him well.

And that's what I did. Mum had put on her brand-new tight-fitting diamond dress and Dad was adjusting his brand-new orange bubble hat. I said goodbye to them, packed some krystalumps and headed for the bus stop. The busmobile came

along in no time and soon I was passing new buildings, their pointed tops covered in fleecy pink
cloud. Beeny hoppers and jetmobiles dotted the sky
and reminded me that my last lesson would be
coming up any time.

'Intergalactic Zoo,' called the driver.

I pushed past squealing kids and jumped off the
bus. There was a big queue for tickets. News of the
latest addition to the Zoo had spread quickly. A
huge sign outside the Zoo announced:

VIEW OUR NEWEST ATTRACTION.

Just arrived from the other side of the universe.
A two-eyed walking animal.

ENTER OUR CONTEST TO NAME THE CREATURE.
Win a free family holiday to Phlotzo
for two hecta-weeks.
Scroll forms are available at the Zoo entrance.

I handed in my hooberoos at the gate and went
inside. All the animals were kept in large super-
glass cages, and they were all well cared for. Some
animals had two eyes and four legs but a two-

legged, two-eyed creature, that was freaky. It would certainly go down well with the crowds.

I passed the green, fire-eating monster. He had stuck his small pointed head into a pot of flames and was about to have breakfast. His eyes gleamed and his long red tail waved in the air.

Then there were the two-headed monsters from Exenia – both heads always arguing with one another and sometimes even biting each other's stubby noses. They had spotted orange bodies and small furry hoofs.

I followed the signs saying, 'This way to the creature from deep space'.

It wasn't hard to find his cage, because there was a big crowd standing around it.

'Look – two eyes! And see those funny expressions on its face. Isn't it amazing? It can run around on its legs like us. And wearing clothing.'

Kids and their parents were chattering and shrieking and pointing. I pushed my way through the crowd, and eventually, by hopping up and down, I managed to see the alien boy.

He was walking around his cage and every now and then he'd stop and stare at the crowd. Then he'd poke a long tongue out of his mouth and do really funny things with his two eyes. Why was he

poking out his tongue? Maybe he was hungry. I looked around his cage. They'd tried to make him comfortable – there was a soft lava bed suspended just above the cage floor, and in front of his bed was a food tray. At the Zoo they are very careful with space creatures' diets. The scientists scan the last meal that the animals have eaten and recreate it in one mushy food brick.

I pushed myself forward – not easy, but a pinch here and a push there and I was at the front. I pressed my face against the cage. The alien boy continued to pull an amazing variety of faces at the crowd.

Suddenly both his eyes focussed on me. He

screwed them up, walked over to the edge of the cage and pressed his hands against the glass. Five fingers on each hand. That was quite a lot. I wondered if the extra finger got in the way.

He was staring right at me, and funny sounds were coming out of his mouth. It sounded like a lot of habble gabble and I didn't have a clue what he was talking about. But then, he couldn't talk. Not really. It was just noise. He had no intelligence. Wasn't that what Dad said? Dad would know. So how come he seemed to recognise me from two days ago? After all, to him, we must have all looked the same. Mustn't we? Now he was jumping up and down. He seemed very excited. Maybe he needed to go to the toilet. That must have been it. No, now he'd stopped jumping and ... oh no, there was something coming out of the corner of his eyes. Blobs of water. So that was it. He had an eye infection. And he only had two eyes. This was serious stuff. I'd better tell the keeper right away.

At the main office I rushed up to a keeper. 'It's the new creature from deep space. He's got blobs of water running down from the sides of his eyes. He must be sick.'

The keeper looked up from his writing. 'Oh, it's you, Tal. Fine specimen your father brought back.

Don't worry about the water. We think it's something to do with stress. He doesn't appear to get a
stress lump on his forehead like we do, but when
he's upset water oozes out the sides of his eyes.
He'll settle down.'

That sounded sad. What if he didn't settle down?

'There's something else,' I said. 'I think he recognised me from when I first saw him at the spaceport. He looked at me in a way that was ... well ...
different.'

'That's not possible, Tal,' the keeper said gently.
'He's an alien boy. We know that much. But you
must also know what your father told you. He has
no intelligence.'

'He made noises with his mouth. It was habble
gabble but maybe some sounds were words.'

The keeper sighed. 'Tal, you're getting carried
away. Now please, I have work to do.'

I wandered back to the alien boy's cage, chewing
on one of Mum's krystalumps. Again, I pushed
through the crowd to get a better view. The boy was
sitting on the cage floor cautiously examining a
food brick. Why was he hesitating before he ate it?
The animals usually took one sniff and scoffed the
lot. After all, it was made up of the same food he'd
normally eat at home.

He took a bite, then another. Great follyfoops, he'd stopped eating and was staring right at me again. Why? Now he was jumping up and down. He did recognise me. He really did. I didn't care what anyone said.

I walked away from the cage feeling confused. Dad said the boy was part of the slave class on his planet – that he wasn't intelligent at all. Why would Dad say that if it wasn't true?

I caught a busmobile home. Mum and Dad weren't back from the Space Academy, so I went straight to my bedroom. It was always in a mess and it drove my parents mad. There were scroll crayons and scrunched bubble suits lying all over the floor, bits of decomposing lava dust and other food scraps, and a squillion other things.

Under my desk I kept my transpeaker. It looked just like an ordinary lingo dish but I'd added things. I might fall asleep in class when we were learning history, and it was hard to keep my eyes open during story writing, but when it came to computers and inventions I was definitely whiz-bang smart. The thing with the transpeaker was that I'd added my own computer program. It was meant to interpret lots of different sounds and tell me the Zordethian equivalents. For example, I bet very few people knew that 'Zrepyt equi-3 ellt?' meant 'Can you show me the way to the toilet before I burst?' in Phonian.

It took me a long time to master the transpeaker, but I was almost ready for its first trial. I adjusted a few enophots on the back of the computer and linked them up to the main power glass.

Then I primed the transmitter and receiver. Their cores were made out of granorock, the very hardest rock you can find on Zordeth. I linked the zeno wires, and checked the circuits. If I'd done this correctly there was a chance I could communicate directly with anyone anywhere in the universe.

It would be gigglegopping if I could communicate with the alien boy. Even if all he could say was, 'Your planet's really off.'

Next time I went to the Zoo I'd take along my recorder and tape his sounds. Then I could feed them into my transpeaker. If it worked I should be able to find out if he was talking or if it was just habble gabble. If it wasn't habble gabble I could get my computer to analyse the sounds and pick up the language strands. That's if it worked. If it didn't work then I'd be as cranky as a cubblecog.

Just then I heard the bubble car pull up. Mum and Dad were home. I dropped everything and ran out to meet them. Dad walked straight up to me and jumped on my feet. 'I've had a splendid day, Tal, just splendid. And guess what? I'm going to be promoted. And I'm going to be on the front page of the *Zordethian Daily News* tomorrow.'

Mum smiled. 'It's been a very hectic day. Veth, let's sit down and relax for a while and you can tell Tal all about it.'

I followed my parents into the cushy-cove room and we hopped into our coves and lay there in silence for a minute while the lava bubbles gently massaged our backs. Dad looked very happy.

'I showed them the pictures of the planet from

deep space, and they were all so impressed they immediately stood up and jumped on each other's feet. It's never happened before. What an honour! That boy will bring huge crowds to the Zoo.'

'Will you be going back to deep space again, Dad?' I asked.

'Well, judging by the reaction I got from the films I showed, I don't think so. The planet I visited was the only inhabited one and the ruling race there are far too warlike. This alien boy is enough to bring crowds flocking back to the Zoo. And Tal, your father's going to be Intergalactic Zoo Director.'

'Zoo Director?' I clicked.

'Isn't it wonderful,' Mum said..

'Great sizzling sentapods – it's fantastic!'

My father just lay there looking contented.

'Dad,' I went on. 'There's something I need to know. That boy at the Zoo – well, I went there today, and I went right up to his cage. I'm almost sure he recognised me.'

'That can't be,' Dad said quickly. He adjusted his bubble hat but not before I noticed a stress lump appearing. 'You're just imagining things, Tal.'

While I thought about this, Dad jumped off his cushy cove, hurried out of the room, then returned with his movie of the far-off planet. This was exciting stuff. We all sat in our coves while Dad focussed the picture on the glass ceiling.

I couldn't believe it. The seas were blue, the skies were blue and the clouds were white! There were tall buildings and strange-looking aliens wearing strange-looking clothes, running around what must have been streets. I saw green, leafy things that must have been alien trees. And what was that strange animal with the long grey trunk? And, oh no, what was that?

Aliens were holding weapons and shooting at each other. How awful. And …things that looked a bit like bubble cars on streets. And that? An alien sticking a sharp blade into another alien and look, red blood coming out. Red blood. How off. How terrible that one alien could do that to another.

Dad was right. They were a truly fierce lot out there. The alien boy might feel a bit out of sorts right now but at least he was away from all that violence.

I shivered. 'What a horrible place,' I said to Dad.

Dad nodded. We watched some more then turned off the recorder. Stress lumps were rising on all our foreheads.

'They have bombs. They hurt each other,' Mum clicked in a sad voice.

'Yes, that is the way of life there,' said Dad. 'These pictures come straight from their news broadcasts.'

'Wasn't there anything good there, Dad?' I asked.

Dad clicked sadly. 'No, I'm afraid not. It's a very violent place and we should stay away. We have our specimen for the Zoo.'

'But what if the alien boy doesn't adjust to the Zoo? He looked ... I don't know ... unhappy. He gets this water coming from the side of his eyes when he's stressed. That's what the keeper told me.'

Dad turned away. 'He'll be all right,' he said. 'Now, I must go to my desk. I have to prepare my acceptance speech for tomorrow. Director!

Middling muddhops, this trip has certainly made me famous.'

I stared at Dad. He was overdoing this fame and glory thing. Still, I guess becoming Director of the Intergalactic Zoo was a big honour.

That night I sat and stared up at the moons. I found myself wondering what the alien boy was doing. Was he looking at the same moons? What was he thinking?

But then, he couldn't think, could he?

CHAPTER

5

Gike returned from holidays after a hecta-week so that gave us some time together before we went back to school. I had so much to tell him. He had so much to tell me.

He came over to my place and we sat in the coves swinging and eating krystalumps.

'I went skimskating right down the mouth of a dormant volcano,' he said. 'It was fintabulous.'

I told him everything that had been happening to me – my dad's trip, the space boy, the way I kept wondering if he was intelligent.

'That's serious stuff,' said Gike, shaking his head. 'If you're right, then that would mean that your dad was breaking the rules, wouldn't it?'

I felt a huge stress lump coming on. I couldn't face up to that.

'Tell you what,' said Gike. 'Let's go to the Zoo. I

want to see this space boy for myself. You can
record the sounds he makes and, if I bring along
my maths assignment, can you help me with it?
You're so good at maths. And I can give you a hand
with your history project if you like.'

'You're on.'

I grabbed my recorder and the history scroll
book, and we collected Gike's maths assignment on
the way to the bus stop. The busmobile was crowd-
ed, and we hung on to the straps and chewed sea-
flavoured gubblebum.

'Intergalactic Zoo,' the driver called, and we got
off along with a huge crowd of parents and kids.

'Looks like the Zoo is doing big business again,'
said Gike.

When we were inside, Gike wanted to have a
look at some of the other space creatures on his
way to see the boy, but I pushed him past the
many-eyed floctypus from Lebus, and past the izud
with its striped tentacles. You couldn't dawdle near
the izud because it spat, and if you stood too close
you came away sopping wet.

When we got to the boy's cage we had to do a lot
of pinching and pushing to squirm our way to the
front of the crowd.

'Squiggling squaghoppers!' Gike clicked when he

saw the boy up close. 'He's, he's ... different.'

The boy was jumping up and down pulling the most incredible range of faces. His tongue was sticking out of his mouth and his eyes were turning somersaults. What did it all mean?

Then the boy gazed around at the crowd and water leaked from the sides of his eyes. He turned and walked to the back of the cage, lay down on his bed and faced the other way.

'I guess he's tired,' said Gike. 'All that jumping and face pulling. It's taken a lot out of him.'

'I think he's just plain miserable,' I said.

The crowd was disappointed. 'I want him to jump and stick his tongue out of his mouth again,' said one little girl.

'I want one for my next birthday,' said some dumb little kid.

'You can't, sweetheart,' said his mother patiently.

'I want him! I want him!' yelled the kid, and then he spun himself around and began to bite his mother, which Zordethian kids like to do when they're having a tantrum.

Eventually the crowd began to thin because they could see so little of the boy. Gike and I stood there.

'Reckon we should sit somewhere and you can look at my maths problems,' said Gike.

I stared at the back of the alien boy as he lay on his bed. I wanted to get his attention. I called out to him, but he didn't respond at all. This way I wouldn't get a chance to record his sounds.

Then suddenly, like a huge bolt of Zordethian lightning, a great idea hit my brain.

'Gike,' I said excitedly, 'if you were on another planet and you had to communicate and you couldn't speak the language, what would you do?'

'I'd go crazy,' said Gike.

'No, Gike, think. If you couldn't make yourself understood you just might be able to communicate with pictures.'

'What are you getting at?'

I tore out some pages from my scroll pad, took

out my scroll crayon and rolled it inside the pages. I fiddled around in my pocket and found a bit of wire, made a neat little parcel, then looked quickly around. Good, there was only one little girl staring at the alien boy's back and she was clicking with disappointment and moving away.

I threw the package over the glass wall of the cage and it landed with a thud. The boy turned around. I noticed that water was still coming out of both his eyes.

Then he saw the package and slowly got off his bed and walked towards it. At the same time I

jumped up and down and called to him.

He looked at me and there was no doubt about it. He knew me. He ran to the wall of the cage and stared at me, talking away in habble gabble. I quickly turned on my recorder while Gike waved his arms and pointed to the scroll pages and crayon.

The boy turned around, still making sounds. He bent and picked up the small package, undid the wire, then stared at the scroll pages and crayon. Then something really odd happened. He picked them up and his mouth curled up into this strange half circle. He showed his teeth, and his eyes curled up into something like a smile.

'What does that mean?' asked Gike. 'Do you think he wants to bite you?'

'No,' I said while I thought about it. 'I'm not exactly sure, but he doesn't have enough eyes to smile properly. I know it's off, but I've got a feeling that he might be smiling with his mouth.'

The boy quickly ran back to his bed and faced the wall, which was just as well because people started to run over to the cage when they saw him moving. He lay facing the wall for ages, while Gike and I wondered what he was doing.

'Maybe he thinks it's food,' said Gike. 'Maybe he'll eat it and get sick.'

Then the boy turned around. There was nobody around but us. People had rushed up to the cage then wandered away looking for some more exciting creatures. He jumped off his bed, wrapped the wire round some scroll paper then threw it over the wall of the cage. I caught it, and Gike and I moved away from the cage to unwrap the scroll paper.

'Oh no!'

The alien boy had drawn a picture. It showed a large ball and nine smaller balls. There was a mark beside one ball.

'It's his planetary system,' I moaned. 'Look – that big round ball must be his sun. Those smaller ones are planets. He's telling us that's where he lives. The one he's marked must be his home planet.'

'Why are you upset? This is very exciting stuff,' grinned Gike. 'And look at those figures.'

The boy had drawn four aliens: two big ones and two smaller ones. They were wearing odd-looking clothing and all had curling mouths.

'It's his family,' I clicked. 'This is terrible. The boy's intelligent and he's being locked up in the Zoo. Why would my father do such a thing?'

Gike went very quiet. He handed me another gubblebum but I waved it aside.

'My dad,' I continued. 'The best in Zordeth. The kindest. Why?'

A king-size stress lump throbbed on my forehead. Gike reached out and touched it.

'You'd better get home and rest, Tal. You're in a bad way.'

I wanted to go back to the boy. I wanted to tell him that I'd help him, though I had no idea how or when. But now I was too sick to do a thing.

We took one last look at the boy before we left the Zoo. People had gathered around his cage and he was lying facing the wall again.

We caught the busmobile home, and Gike got out a few stops before me. 'Don't worry,' he whispered, 'we'll think of something'.

At home, I put my recorder in my bedroom.

Later I'd see if I could make anything out of the boy's weird sounds. But now I felt too sick. I went straight to the cushy-cove room and sat for hecta-hours in the cove, allowing the fine lava bubbles to knead the back of my head and neck. Every now and then I touched my aching stress lump – it wasn't going down. I felt totally off.

Mum came home from work and found me in the cove.

'What's up, Tal? You've turned pale blue.'

I couldn't tell her. I just couldn't. I had to have it out with Dad first.

He arrived home just before dinner. He was singing to himself and while I was sure it would do great things for our space flowers it did nothing for me.

He'd brought home the afternoon paper and I could hear him say proudly to Mum, 'Look, you have a famous husband. Who knows, soon we can move to a bigger house. We'll have everything we've ever wanted. We can go for holidays to all those exotic planets you've wanted to visit.'

He blah blahed on and on. Mum must have said something to him, because the next thing I knew he was standing over me in the cushy-cove room. All his eyes were filled with worry.

'Tal,' he said. 'What's going on? Your mother told me you aren't well. Good goggle! That's a huge stress lump.'

I turned my head away and stared at our rainbow wall.

'Tal,' said Dad, and this time he gently touched the lump and began to massage it. 'Come on, it can't be that bad.'

So I let it all out. 'Dad – how could you, my own dad, the best dad in all the universe. You've locked up a thinking being. You must have known. Look. He drew this.'

I reached into my pocket and pulled out the alien boy's pictures. I almost threw them at my father. He took them and stared at them for a long time. Then he staggered to the cove beside mine and lay down in it.

'What really happened in deep space? Please tell me the truth.'

My father shook his head and punched himself hard. When he turned to me his voice was very quiet.

'Tal, you know the situation I was in. My job, everything I had worked for, was at stake. I needed something to bring the crowds back to the Zoo. I needed something different.'

'Just tell me, did you know he was an intelligent being?'

Dad stared at the ceiling. He stared at the walls. He punched himself again, then said, 'Yes, I knew.'

'Tell me everything. I have to know.'

Mum walked in then. She'd been hanging around outside the door listening. She didn't say a word, just grabbed a cove and the three of us lay there, our faces pale blue with lumps bulging on our foreheads. Two of Dad's eyes looked at me. The others focussed on Mum. He began his story.

'It's a strange world – awful in some ways, yes, but not in others.'

'Is it true that there's a slave race there?' I asked.

'No,' said Dad slowly. He turned away, looking as miserable as a hungry heno. 'There were many, many people squeezed onto the planet. Some were different colours, some had different-shaped eyes, although no one had more than two. I watched their news programs on my video screen. You saw the buildings. And yes, in some places there was war, and people did terrible things to each other.'

Dad hesitated. He took out a scroll tissue and wiped his forehead. 'However, there were good things too. Aliens towing a large creature out to sea when it had become stuck in shallow water. People in trouble helping each other. Poor thin-looking aliens being fed by others. Aliens standing in front of trees trying to stop them being chopped down.'

Dad punched himself again. 'Yes, there were good things. I shouldn't have taken the boy. He was alone in an open area, running, kicking a large object with his feet. I had to act quickly. There were larger animals, but they weren't accessible. Too big or similar in some way to our own space creatures. Also the engine in the spaceship was giving trouble. I needed to act fast.

'The boy walked upright. He wore clothing. All this was amazing. I was worried. My job. What would become of us if I lost it? I thought maybe I could send the boy back after a while, when interest in the Zoo was restored. I'd find a way. I didn't mean to keep him forever.'

And with that my dad went into a complete stress collapse. Another lump appeared on his forehead and no amount of massaging would calm him down.

'I have brought shame to my family,' he wailed.

Mum couldn't say a word. She was too shocked. 'A little boy. Like Tal. With a fine intelligent mind. Trapped here. Oh, Veth.'

I got up from my cushy cove and stormed out of the room. I didn't care if Dad sprouted another six stress lumps. He deserved every one of them. I went to my room. I had to think of a plan.

CHAPTER

When I got to my room I remembered the sounds I'd taped on my recorder. I linked it up to my transpeaker, feeling a bit nervous. If it worked, if ... I turned a few knobs, plugged in a lead and adjusted a dial. There was no way it would work. No way. Surely ...

A muffled sound came out of the transpeaker, wobbly and distorted. Then I heard garbled noises which made no sense. Well, I hadn't really expected it to work.

Then ...

'Help me. Get me out of here. I remember you. You're the little blue creep I saw the first day I got here. Help me find a way back to Earth. You must. My name's Max. Please ... '

Then there was more garbled noise. Then ... 'You want me to write something? Good. Perhaps then you'll understand that I don't belong here.'

Great fires of Phonia. I felt my eyes rolling around in my head with shock. He was talking and his name was Max. I had to help him.

Then I remembered the transpeaker. I'd done it! I'd made, all by myself, a super sintillectical inter-galactic lingo dish. Me. Tal! The one who was always sent to the back of the class to hop and jump around because I daydreamed.

I turned off the recorder and lay down on my bed. I'd speak to Gike tomorrow. Together we'd work out a plan.

Meantime, my brain was rattling around like a biller in a bopper. I'd never get to sleep. I'd never sleep again. I'd ... zzzzz.

When I woke up the next day Dad had already left for work. Mum was sitting at the kitchen table drinking sunrise tea.

She looked up as I came in. 'Help yourself to some stone crispies,' she said in a flat voice. Then she added, 'Tal, try not to be too hard on your father. We'll find a way around this. But it's going to take time and thought.'

I staggered to a bubble chair and pushed the packet of crispies away. 'I'm not hungry. I may never be hungry again. How would you feel if I was spacenapped? Because that's what Dad's done. He's spacenapped that alien boy. How'd you be? You'd be running around diffing and duffing and all the time I'd be in some weirdo zoo on the other side of the universe.'

Mum leant over and stroked my forehead. 'I understand how you feel,' she said. 'And we will try to think of something. In the meantime I'm going to see the boy at the Zoo. I've only got one class today. I'll take him some of my krystalumps. Maybe that will cheer him up.'

I shook my head. My mum was nuts. 'Don't you know you can't feed the animals at the Zoo? Not even that boy. He can't eat our food. He eats some horrible stuff that's been processed into a Zordethian brick. Your krystalumps would kill him.'

Mum looked troubled. 'Well, I want to see him anyway. Maybe there's some way I can make life easier for him.'

There was a thump on the door. 'That's probably Gike,' said Mum. 'He came round earlier but you were still asleep. I'll let him in – you eat your breakfast.'

I sat miserably at the kitchen table. My stomachs growled. Maybe I'd just have a small plate of stone crispies. It'd help me concentrate on ways to help the space boy, Max. Max – a funny name. Yes, I'd find a way to help him. Gike came into the kitchen, and I heard Mum call out, 'I'm off to the Zoo. Now behave, you two, and don't muck around.'

'Yes, Mum, sure, Mum, no, Mum,' I said.

As soon as she'd gone I took Gike into my bedroom. He listened to my transpeaker and he turned pale blue with shock.

'I can hardly believe my ears. Even the ones in my feet are wriggling with amazement. He talks. And you, you're a total genius, Tal, even if you don't know one end of history from the other. Can we communicate with him?'

'No worries,' I said confidently.

After working for several hecta-hours I'd fed the entire Zordethian language into my computer, and translated it into all the sounds that made up Max's language. I'd also adapted three mini lingo dishes so they could work off the transpeaker. There were two switches at the bottom of each lingo dish … lingo dish – what a boring name for something that would help us speak across galaxies.

'I'm calling these beeper squeakers,' I told Gike. 'You press that one to speak and that one to listen. We'll give one to Max and that way we can have a proper conversation with him.'

'But what are we going to do about getting him home? Have you read today's paper?'

'What's that got to do with anything?'

Gike reached into his pocket and pulled out a folded newspaper. 'Read this,' he said.

I saw the headline first – 'Concern Over Latest Space Creature' – then I grabbed the paper from Gike and read out loud:

There is widespread concern at the Intergalactic Zoo about the latest space creature. The creature, now named Phlexyglot as a result of the recent 'Name the creature contest', is showing signs of distress. He spends much of his time curled up on his rest pad and eats very little food.

'Well,' I said to Gike. 'What do they expect?'

'Have you spoken to your dad?'

I quickly told Gike about my confrontation with my father. I was so distressed I began to punch myself.

'Dad knows he's done the wrong thing, but he's so caught up with being Intergalactic Zoo Director I reckon he's scared he'll get into serious trouble. He's in no hurry to work out a way to take the boy back.'

'Well, something's got to be done soon,' said Gike. 'Finish the article.'

I looked back at the article and read on.

The space creature, Phlexyglot, was brought back to Zordeth by eminent zoologist Veth Xofloat with the aid of a new gigadrive spacecraft. Recently a fault has been found in the fuel drive and scientists now believe that future trips to the far side of the universe are unlikely.

I put down the newspaper. 'Great bells of banglee. This is terrible. Max may be stuck here for the rest of his life!'

Much later, after Mum had come back from the Zoo and made all kinds of miserable clicking sounds about Max, Gike and I said we were going for a walk.

'That sounds nice,' said Mum, as she staggered into the cushy-cove room.

Gike and I put our beeper squeakers in our pockets, and I carried the extra one for Max. Then we hopped on a busmobile to the Zoo.

We got there quite late, but the usual crowds were hanging around Max's cage. When he first arrived and pulled faces, everyone was amazed. Now people shook their heads and said things like, 'The trip across the universe was obviously too much for him. He must be very sick.'

Of course he was sick – homesick. That's what.

The crowds came and went and eventually there was a moment when nobody else was around. Gike and I crept right up to Max's cage. I called out to him, but he just lay on his bed. I called again. He turned his head around slowly and started to poke his tongue out of his mouth, but I had no idea what that meant.

When he saw it was us he jumped off the bed and came running to the edge of the cage. I wrapped the beeper squeaker in my old bubble hat and tossed it over the glass wall. He caught it and quickly unwrapped it. Then he showed me his teeth – he had a lot of them – and curled his mouth. I smiled back. Then Gike pointed excitedly to the switches down the bottom. He took out his own beeper squeaker and flicked on the switch.

In his best Zordethian he said, 'My name is Gike.'

Max fiddled with a switch. He turned on one, then the other, and I saw him jump back in shock.

A flood of sounds came from his mouth. Quickly I turned on my receiving button.

'I can understand you,' he said, in what came out as a low-pitched Zordethian voice. 'You've got to help me.' Then he looked at me. 'And you're ... '

'Tal,' I said.

We stood there for a moment staring at each other. 'My father's the one who brought you here,'

I told him sadly. Then I punched myself. He looked surprised at that, but I hoped it showed him how bad I felt about it. 'He's done the wrong thing, but somehow Gike and I are going to find a way to get you home.'

Max's mouth curled into a big smile. 'Good,' he said.

'You're so tall,' said Gike staring at him. 'Taller than my dad even. It's fintabulous.'

Max screwed up his forehead. 'What does that mean?'

I twisted a few knobs at the bottom of my beeper squeaker. Could it translate fintabulous?

A funny word came through Max's beeper squeaker. He listened then said, 'You mean awesome. I'm so tall it's awesome. Well, not where I come from. I'm just average. My dad's heaps taller than me. What's that thing you do with your eyes? It looks painful.'

'It's a smile,' I said. 'Like what you do with your mouth, I think.'

Just then I heard someone call out, 'Hey, what's going on here?'

I knew that voice.

'Go quickly to your bed. Lie down. Find a place to hide the beeper squeaker,' I told Max in a rush. Great Zordethian zillybumps!

Max ran to his bed, lay down and faced the wall. Gike and I turned around. It was Fiz, the mean, horrible space scientist who hated kids.

'Tal,' he said. 'What a surprise to see you here so late in the day. Isn't this your friend Gike? I believe I've met him at your home.'

Gike nodded his head. He looked at me with two of his eyes and stared at Fiz with the other two.

Fiz said loudly, 'What exactly was going on here? I'd been under the impression that the space boy was ill. He rarely leaves his bed. But I saw him quite clearly jumping around and he was holding something in his hand. What was it?'

'A food brick,' I said quickly. 'I, um, encouraged him to eat his food.'

'But that jumping. He looked quite healthy from a distance. It seems to me there was more than that going on here.'

He stared at both of us. Two eyes focussed on Gike and two on me. We didn't say a word.

'Anyway, I'll be round at your house tonight, Tal. I want to have a chat with your father. He's so busy now with his new elevated job it's hard to catch up with him. I'll see you later.'

Fiz took one more look at Max then walked away.

As we left the Zoo, Gike said, 'That Fiz has a mean face,' which was the understatement of the hecta-year.

CHAPTER

7

That night, after dinner, when Dad was brewing rock oil and Mum was sketching something in her scroll pad, Fiz, the most unpleasant person on Zordeth, arrived.

He thumped on our door and when Dad let him in he was obviously in a din-dandy mood. I was sure he was jealous of Dad. He'd been hoping to be made Zoo Director and Dad said when he heard that he'd missed out on the job he'd freaked.

He and Dad went to the cushy-cove room, lay in the coves and talked. I barged in, pretending to get a scroll book from the cupboard.

'Doesn't the boy have other things to do?' asked Fiz. I twisted all my eyes into a big glare. Dad said, 'Tal, Fiz and I have things to discuss. Take a new scroll book and leave us alone.'

'Sure thing,' I said, but of course I hung around

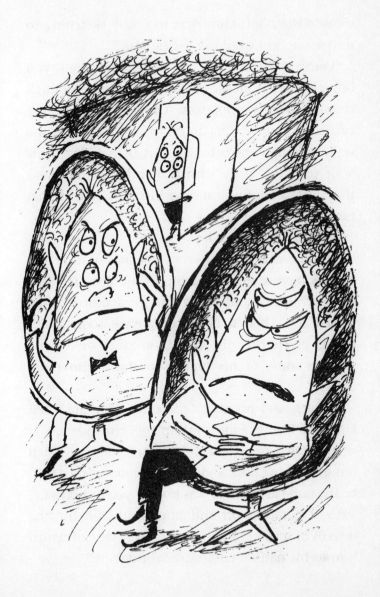

outside the door. Mum was too busy sketching to notice me, so I wouldn't get caught.

'Veth,' I heard Fiz say. 'This specimen you brought back from the far side of the universe – he's certainly very unresponsive. Crowds are dwindling again. He simply curls up on his bed and faces the wall. I thought he was sick. But then today I saw your son, Tal, there with a friend. I could swear they were communicating with the alien. Is that possible?'

My father clicked a low, 'No'.

'Hmm,' said Fiz. 'Anyway, the fact is that the crowds have stopped coming to the Zoo. The boy has not turned out to be the attraction we had hoped for. There'll be a conference soon and I think, given that the boy is unique, we should remove some of his organs to study him more closely.'

'What?' said my dad. 'You can't do that. You'll kill him. That is a most inhumane, cruel idea.'

Fiz's voice grew louder. 'We won't kill him. We'll put everything back and there's a good chance he'll be the same as before. I was hoping you'd cooperate, Veth. Operating on the boy would be for the benefit of science, and there's no way we can return him to his natural environment now.'

'I'll have no part in it,' said my father and I knew without looking he must have had a gigantic stress lump on his forehead.

'It will be put to a vote,' said Fiz, and he sounded angry.

My father suddenly said, 'What if you were to find out that the boy was a thinking creature? What then?'

'Then you'd be in big trouble, Veth,' said Fiz, and I could imagine all his eyes shining wickedly. 'Imagine analysing the brain of a thinking creature from the far side of the universe. There would be so much to learn. But then of course he's not a thinking creature, is he?'

My father was silent. Just then there was a tap on my shoulder.

'Tal, what are you doing hanging around here? If you have so much time to spare go and sing to my flowers.'

Mum was staring at me. 'Yes, Mum. Sure,' I said, but when she'd turned away I ran to my bedroom. I threw myself on my bed to think. This was serious stuff. Even if my dad did confess his wrong-doing there was no guarantee that he could stop Fiz.

Imagine Max sprawled out on a crystal operating table while scientists prodded and probed.

I heard the front door close with a thud. Fiz had gone. I ran to the cushy-cove room. Dad was still sitting there, clutching his hands and looking very upset.

'I heard everything, Dad,' I told him. 'What are you going to do?'

'I don't know, Tal. There doesn't seem to be an answer. Even if I tell the truth there are still those who would use the boy for experiments. After all, it's most unlikely that we can ever return to that side of the universe.'

I sat on the floor next to Dad. 'What's wrong with the new spaceship? Why can't you go back?'

'It's the fuel drive, Tal. It has to supply an enormous burst of power when we go into gigadrive. I think there's probably enough power to get it back to the boy's planet but there's just no guarantee it could return. We've tried to fix it, but there's something very wrong with it.'

'Isn't there any way to get it to work?'

'Maybe if we reduced the weight of the ship – but no, it's too risky, Tal,' said Dad. 'Now please, leave me alone. I need to sit here and feel guilty.' Dad punched himself hard.

Just before I went to bed that night Mum reminded me, 'Tal, you still haven't had your final flying lesson. San contacted me today. I booked you in for tomorrow. Okay?'

I was about to say I couldn't care less about my final flying lesson, but then another bolt of Zordethian lightning struck my brain. 'Yes, Mum. Sure thing, Mum.'

Mum stared at me. 'Well, I'm glad to see that you're smiling again, Tal. Try not to worry about the boy. It's very sad but I don't think there's anything we can do right now.'

The next day Gike came over. We hung around the front garden clicking away to each other in low voices.

'Today I'm having my final flying lesson,' I told Gike. 'After that I'll know everything there is to know about whiz-banging around the galaxy.'

'That's not going to help Max,' Gike clicked sadly.

'I've got an idea. It's not just any idea. It's a fintabulous sintillectical idea. That's if it works.'

Gike's ears curled up with interest. 'Tell me about it.'

CHAPTER

When I woke up the next day I jumped out of bed and dressed quickly. There was a lot to do and not much time.

Dad was just about to leave for work. His face was very strained with his eyes curled into a wobbly sad expression.

'I'm going to tell the Space Academy the truth, Tal,' he said. 'This has gone too far.'

Suddenly I felt sorry for him. He'd done wrong but he was still my dad. I went up to him and jumped lightly on his bright orange shoes.

I wanted to tell him that I was absolutely positive everything was going to be okay. But then he might ask questions. After giving himself a final punch in the chest, Dad squeezed my nose and left.

Over breakfast I told Mum, 'I'm off to the spaceport just as soon as I've finished eating.'

'That's fine, Tal,' she said. 'On the way to the bus stop can you buy me some space-flower seeds? I want to plant a few in the back garden. Perhaps they'll cheer us up.' Mum looked past me deep in thought. I could imagine how all this was getting to her.

I bought a packet of space-flower seeds from Zop Jonx at our local shop. I didn't like her very much. She told me off the last time I came in because I made a smell. The shop windows were closed and I had just eaten seven krystalumps in a row. I didn't mean to do it. It could have happened to anyone.

As I went into the shop, I saw all her eyes darting around checking that the windows were open. I quickly handed her the hooberoos and grabbed some space-flower seeds. It was disgusting. She was already sniffing. I pushed the seeds to the bottom of my pocket and rushed out of the shop. Then I ran to catch the busmobile to the spaceport.

When I arrived I went straight up to San's room. He was a short, skinny guy with wisps of curly orange hair peeping out from under his green hat. There was a stamp on the hat with a picture of a jet-mobile on it, just to let everyone know he was an instructor.

'You're bright and early,' he said. 'Well, let's begin.'

I followed him onto the spacefield, across the lines of jetmobiles and beeny hoppers.

'Your jetmobile is over there.' San pointed to a small silver craft.

I felt very excited. Soon I'd know all there was to know. Soon ...

We walked across the warm red spacefield.

'Where's my dad's spaceship?' I asked San.

San stroked his little blue chin. 'Hmm, let me see. Yes, there it is. On pad XXS.'

He pointed. It was quite small and similar to a dozen others around it.

'Um, Dad wants you to show me how his ship works. You know, how to get into gigadrive to get to the other side of the universe.'

San stopped walking. He stared at Dad's craft then at me.

'That's odd. Doesn't he want to show you himself?'

'He's so busy since he's been made Zoo Director. He thought you wouldn't mind, seeing you were with me today anyway.'

'Mind? Of course I don't mind. Sizzling sozzlesumps – your father is an important man. It's an honour to be of assistance. But we'll finish your last space lesson first.'

As we reached the jetmobile, San took a metal disc from his pocket.

'My master key.' He smiled. 'Just as well I'm not dishonest, isn't it? This opens just about anything.'

'That's nice,' I murmured.

We climbed the metal staircase and, once inside, San sat on a cloud seat at the front of the jetmobile. I sat beside him facing the controls. The ship was very small – just enough room for the two of us.

'Now, Tal,' said San. 'This is your final lesson. You have to show me that you can adequately navigate and control the ship, then listen while I explain a little more about intergalactic travel. If I am satisfied that you've obtained the necessary knowledge and skills, you'll be qualified to drive your own jet-mobile.'

San asked me questions and I went over everything I'd ever learnt. I blah blahed on and on. He seemed pleased, nodded his head and ticked a report scroll. Then I slowly adjusted the controls. We checked with the space tower then I lifted the craft off the ground. Soon my ship was high above the pink fluffy clouds. Another turn of the dial and we were out of the Zordethian atmosphere and in space.

It was wonderful. The sky was filled with a squillion stars. I passed the two silver moons of Zordeth, turned the craft this way and that then charted a course to the nearest planet, landing there under thick cloud. I took off, plotted a course for another planet and went through the same routine again.

San asked lots of questions and wrote things down on his report scroll. Finally he said, 'I just want to explain a little more about intergalactic travel and then you'll have learnt everything I can teach you. You are a credit to your parents. Your father is a great pilot and navigator and I can see that you will be too.'

San then explained how I could chart my way to the end of the galaxy while I listened carefully.

We headed back to Zordeth and I touched down smoothly. San clicked, 'Very good. I am pleased. You've satisfied all my requirements and shown fine skills as a pilot.'

'Great,' I said. 'Now, can we please go and look at my dad's spaceship?'

San glanced at his hecta-watch. 'All right. I've got a little time to spare, but we'd better be quick.'

We climbed down the stairs of my jetmobile and made our way to Dad's spaceship. It looked so ordinary – there was no way you'd guess that it was fitted with the latest technology.

San used his disc key to open the side panel and we climbed inside. I looked around. The only thing that made it different was the cage. That was where the space animals were kept. My stomachs rolled as I thought of how terrified Max must have felt.

'Are the controls on this ship the same as those on the spacemobile?'

'Of course,' said San. 'The only difference is this lever here. When you reach a speed of 45 000 hecta-vecs you pull it hard. The craft passes through a time and space warp and, cabolla cabang, you arrive at the other side of the universe. This spaceship is the only one fitted with such a function. What a shame there are problems with the fuel drive.'

'But there's still a chance it could work, isn't there, San? If the vessel didn't weigh as much I think that the fuel drive might work. Say you dumped that cage over there and threw out that cabinet. That weighs a fair bit. What d'you reckon?'

San's eyes moved together as he concentrated. 'Of course, that's a possibility. But everything here is necessary for a zoo probe. No, the risk is too great. The spaceship won't be used again.'

San checked his hecta-watch. 'Now, is there anything else you want to know, because I have another student waiting for a lesson?'

'No, I think that just about covers it all,' I clicked.

We left the spaceship and San locked it carefully.

'Can I have a quick look at your disc key?' I asked.

San handed it to me. 'Certainly.'

I took it then squinted my eyes and stared into the distance.

'Isn't that someone waving at you?'

'Where?' San asked. He turned his eyes in all directions. I quickly popped the disc inside the top of my suit.

'I can't see anyone.'

'I must be mistaken,' I said.

We continued walking then San remembered.

'My disc key. You've still got it.'

'Didn't I give it back to you?'

'Of course you didn't. You asked to look at it but you didn't return it. Where is it?'

'Jiggling jugglebeans. I must have dropped it.'

San was very angry. 'I've got no time to waste looking for it, Tal. You go back and find it right away.'

'But I can't,' I said. 'I've, um, got a, um very bad pain in my side. It must be a space cramp. I think I'd better go home and lie down.' I ducked behind the lines of beeny hoppers and jetmobiles and started to run. When I turned around I could see that San had turned dark blue. He was bending down growling, 'That stupid boy. What has he done with my disc key?'

CHAPTER 9

I caught the next busmobile home. I had the disc key safe in my pocket and it was supposed to open just about anything. I hoped that was true.

When I arrived home Gike was already there. He'd been hanging around the front garden near the space flowers talking to Mum. I hoped she hadn't asked him to sing to them.

'Tal,' Gike called. He ran to me. 'How was your lesson? Did everything go okay?'

'Fine,' I said. I walked with Gike up to where Mum was standing. She still looked very worried and even her wriggly curls couldn't hide the stress lump.

'I'm a pilot, Mum,' I told her. 'I'm now qualified to fly my very own jetmobile.'

Mum immediately jumped on both my feet and squeezed my nose. 'Congratulations! Now come inside. I've just made a new batch of krystalumps. We can eat them with a cup of rock brew.'

Gike and I followed her to the kitchen. We sat down and munched and crunched. I hoped San wasn't in a hurry to complain to my parents about me losing his disc. If he could just wait a day or two it would be a big help.

'I'm home.' It was Dad, opening the front door. Mum immediately left the kitchen and I heard them talking quietly to each other, wisping and wasping away.

'Quickly, tell me,' said Gike.

I told him everything and we made plans to meet later. Gike stuffed a few krystalumps into his mouth, said a quick goodbye and left.

Dad came into the kitchen just as Gike shut the back door. Mum didn't even notice he'd gone. She poured Dad a cup of rock brew while I counted the stress lumps on his forehead. Seven. How awful. It would definitely not be a good time for San to phone my parents to complain about me.

'I'm very pleased you have your licence, Tal,' Dad said slowly. 'I'm sorry we can't celebrate but I've had a very worrying day.'

Just then the speakphone squealed. My hearts thumped faster. I was sure it was San.

'I think we'll just ignore the phone,' said Mum.
'We don't need any more habble gabble.'

Phew! Saved.

'Finish your rock brew, Veth, and then you can
have a lie down in your cushy cove,' she added.

And that's what Dad did. Mum lay down in hers,
too, while I sat beside them on the glass floor.

'Want to talk about it, Dad?'

Dad's forehead was a mass of lumps.

'Leave your father alone for now, Tal,' said Mum.

'No, I want to talk. I want Tal to know,' said Dad.

He sighed then spoke. 'I told them the truth –
the members of the Space Academy, the Intergalactic
Zoo authorities. I told everyone. They all know

what a rotten man I am.' My father stopped to punch himself. 'I am no longer Director of the Zoo. I have been demoted to junior space zoologist.'

'Don't let it worry you,' said Mum. 'You had that position when we were first married and you were very happy flipping and flopping around the galaxy.'

'And the boy?' I asked quickly.

'Let me tell you that Fiz was very insistent. He wanted to dissect the alien child and use him for experiments. He said we'd never get another chance to examine a thinking creature from the far side of the universe. Of course, he was out-voted. No decision has yet been made on what to do with the boy. He's going to stay at the Zoo for the time being while we think things out.'

'Maybe he can stay with us,' Mum suggested.

'I think he just wants to go home,' I clicked. 'His family must be out of their brains worrying about him.'

'Not yet,' said Dad. 'According to my calculations and the time warp we went through they may not miss him for some time. Anyway, that's not the point. I am very worried about Fiz. When I left the Academy he was extremely angry. I'm afraid he may still harm the boy.'

Great gizzdingling dallyhops! This was a big
worry, and I had a lot of things to do. I nicked into
Dad's office. It was a big room with pictures of
exotic alien life on the crystal ceilings and walls.
On Dad's wavy rainbow desk were lots of scroll
pads with Dad's wriggly, squiggly writing all over
them.

'Where does he keep it?' I clicked to myself.

I pushed the papers to one side. No, not there. I

opened the marble drawers on the wall. In the very bottom one I found it – a stunner gun. Dad had showed me how it worked, once, and I just might need it. Under the stunner gun were some neatly folded space charts. I quickly studied them. They showed just where Dad had landed when he reached Max's planet.

I quickly shoved the gun and maps inside my suit. Just in time – Mum had walked into the room.

'What are you doing here, Tal? You know you're not supposed to come in here without Dad's permission.'

'I, um, just wanted to see the pictures of all the different creatures he's caught for the Zoo.'

Mum frowned. 'You've seen them lots of times. Don't you have a history assignment to catch up on?'

'Yes, Mum. Sure, Mum. Whatever you say, Mum.'

I left the room quickly and ran to the kitchen. I could hear Mum walking back to the cushy-cove room, so I grabbed handfuls of krystalumps and stuffed them into my pockets. In my bedroom I packed the transpeaker and the two beeper squeakers then sat on my bed planning what to do next.

The evening sky was full of bright stars and the two moons of Zordeth floated silently across it.

Mum, Dad and I had had our dinner, although none of us was particularly hungry. Mum and Dad were talking. I'd told them I wanted to go to bed early. Normally, they'd send for the medic-doc if I suggested such a thing, but tonight they just quietly jumped on my feet and pinched my nose.

After I'd gone to my room I checked my pockets once more: stunner gun, maps, krystalumps ... What was that underneath the krystalumps? The space-flower seeds. Oh well, they could stay there. I'd give them to Mum later. I checked the bulge in my bubble suit: transpeaker, beeper squeakers – I was ready to go. Quietly, I opened my window and jumped out. Gike had better be on time.

I ran quickly to the busmobile station. The service was a bit slack at night. I hung around waiting for Gike and started to panic when I saw the busmobile rolling along, but at that moment Gike came rushing up.

'Couldn't get away,' he said. 'My sister, Zordeth's greatest pain, threw a tantrum. She began to bite my mother. Then she started on me. I jumped out of the window. Widdling wollyhoppers, you are so lucky you don't have a sister.'

We climbed onto the busmobile. It was nearly empty. The driver was surprised when we asked to be dropped off at the Zoo. 'It closes in just ten hecta-minutes,' he warned.

We didn't answer, just grabbed some seats and chewed gubblebum. When the busmobile arrived at the Zoo, we jumped off and made our way to the entrance.

'We're finished for the day,' said the lady at the ticket counter.

'I've, um, lost my favourite bubble hat. Can't you please, please let me in? I'll only be a hecta-minute.'

She hesitated. 'Well, okay, but you'll have to leave by the back exit. I'm closing up here.'

We rushed inside. There was no one around. We ran past the fingals of Phonia, past the many-eyed floctypus, past the spitting izud until ...

Great squiggling squaghoppers! Standing in front of Max's cage and looking as mean as a munchie in a hailstorm was Fiz. Max was lying on his bed facing the wall and Fiz was talking to him. Which just showed what an idiot he was because Max couldn't understand a word.

'You can face the wall and pretend to be stupid. But I know you're not, little space boy. You don't have to be afraid. All I want to do is have a good look inside your head. Study your brain. I won't hurt you, and I'll put everything back again carefully. As carefully as I can, anyway.'

Then he laughed. It was a horrible laugh. His eyes must have been bulging out of their sockets.

Gike and I hid behind the thick branches of a feather tree.

Fiz spun around, looking in all directions. Then he reached into his pocket. He took out a small disc key and his stunner gun.

'He's going to zap Max,' I hissed.

There was no time to do anything but rush at Fiz. He heard us and turned around in surprise, but before he could speak or move I'd zapped him. He stood there, stunner gun in hand, with strands of orange hair standing up on his head like bits of wire.

Gike laughed. I gave him a beeper squeaker and then I called out to Max. 'It's us. Get ready to be rescued.'

I threw a beeper squeaker over the top of the cage. He caught it, gave a weird smile and switched it on.

'About time,' he said with relief. 'I took one look at that creep and jumped into bed. There was something about him ...'

My friend from the far side of the universe was very smart – he knew a creep when he saw one.

'I'm going with Gike to the back of your cage. I reckon I can get it open,' I said.

We left Fiz frozen there with his mouth wide open in suspended horror. I inserted San's disc key in the slot that opened the back of Max's cage. It must work. It must. But what if it didn't?

What a relief! The cage slid open and Max came rushing out.

'Free,' he said. 'I'm free.' He grabbed my arm.

'Now show me the way to get home.'

His skin felt soft, and a bit weird. And it was pinky-brown – ugh. He stood there and I stared up at him. He was so tall, so different. How did he see with just two eyes? What was his home planet really like? Would I ever get to see it?

'We're going to have to make our own way to the spaceport,' Gike told Max. 'It's not that far from here, but there's no way we can take you on the busmobile without the driver having a total stress collapse.'

We rushed past Fiz. He was totally zapped, but I had no idea how long the zapping would last. One thing was certain, we had to get going.

The Zoo was almost deserted. We ran past cages and occasionally we heard Max say, 'Wow!' Translated into Zordethian it meant, 'Great ziggling zamburgers.'

Every now and then we had to quickly dodge a late worker. We hid behind feather trees, which were everywhere, or darted behind cages. Eventually we found a side exit. I pressed a lever, a glass door slid across, and cabolla cabang, we were out.

We ran down the road. 'It's warm!' said Max. 'How do you do that?'

'Lava,' I told him. But there wasn't much time to

talk. We had to be careful. We hid behind as many feather trees as we could find along the way. It wasn't easy. Max was big and a very strange colour, but fortunately, because it was a dark night and we stayed away from the main roads, we weren't seen.

The spaceport was a problem. A lot of workers had gone home, but there were still a few walking around. We nicked along the side of the spaceport, climbed over a tall marble wall, and then it was a matter of trying to find Dad's spaceship.

Luckily, I remembered that it was pretty close to where I had my lesson. Over this line, around there, behind that spacecraft, turn right at that line of beeny hoppers and ...

'That's it. That's Dad's ship.' I said.

We stopped in front of it. We were all exhausted.

'Come quickly,' I beeped Max.

I pressed a silver panel near the side door of the craft. Nothing happened. My disc key. Where was it? I fished under the space charts, moved a few krystalump crumbs to one side. There it was.

I put the shiny disc key into a small slot and a panel in the spaceship's wall slid across.

'Quick,' I said to the others. 'We've got work to do.' We clambered inside and I looked around. 'We've got to dump as much as we can,' I told

them. 'This ship won't make it to the far side of the universe and back unless we can make it as light as possible. At least, that's what I'm counting on. So let's throw out the cage, and that scroll cabinet over there, and even that food chiller.'

Together we started to push and heave and shove and eventually we got everything off the spacecraft. The cage was a problem. It was heavy and too big to fit through the side door.

'What's this?' said Max. He pointed to a small red button at the bottom of the cage, then pressed it. Great bells of banglee! He'd done it. The cage slotted one bar into another until it was the size of a floddle on a rainy day.

Max dropped it outside the spaceship.

'What now?' he asked. Gike stood there awkwardly. Two of his eyes focussed on me, the others on Max.

'Wish I could come too,' he said. 'I'd give anything. But Tal's the expert and he says unless the spaceship is light it's not going to be able to make the trip. So I reckon I'll say goodbye.'

He walked awkwardly over to Max and jumped on his feet. Max looked surprised. 'What was that?' he asked.

'It's a ... ' I fiddled with the controls on my beeper squeaker. 'It's a hug.'

'Goodbye, Gike,' said Max. 'I won't forget you.'

'I won't forget you either,' said Gike, looking very sad. 'Good luck, Tal.'

He climbed out of the spaceship massaging a

stress lump and slid the door shut.

'Well, this is it,' I said to Max. 'Strap yourself into that cloud seat and hang on. We're on our way.'

I was about to lift off when I heard a voice come through my transceiver.

'Tal, it's Dad. Tal, whatever are you doing?'

Oh no, and then, 'It's Mum. Tal, you mustn't, you can't take off in that ship. You'll never make it home. Please ... '

They'd caught up with me. But I couldn't stop, I just couldn't. I hesitated then spoke into the transceiver.

'Mum, Dad, I have to try. I have to get Max home. Don't you understand? He doesn't belong here. Don't worry. I've dumped a lot of useless stuff from the ship and I reckon that with less weight to carry, I'll make it there and back. I'll be okay.'

'Tal, don't do this.' It was Dad. 'I should have realised you were up to something. San phoned. Then there was a call from the Zoo. Fiz was found zapped, holding a stunner gun outside the boy's cage. He's blaming you and claiming that you took the alien. Tal, please get out of the spaceship now. Don't take this risk. You mustn't. You're in great danger.'

'Dad, it's a risk I have to take. Mum, bake some

krystalumps for me for when I return. Goodbye.'

And with that I adjusted my controls, the spaceship rose slowly above the ground, then Max and I shot into the twinkling night sky above Zordeth.

CHAPTER

10

I took a quick look at Max sitting next to me. Both his eyes were staring out the control window.

'Wow!' he said. 'This is totally awesome.'

'Yes,' I said. 'It's ziggling amazing. Each time I fly into space it's as exciting as it was the first time.'

We passed the moons of Zordeth, and soon the seven planets that circled our small sun were left behind. Max asked lots of questions. He wanted to know all about life on Zordeth and the other planets. He was as curious as, as well, as I'd have been if I'd been spacenapped.

'If things had only been different,' he said to me. 'If I could have just come here for my school holidays instead of being spacenapped. It would have been such fun.'

'I could have shown you round Zordeth. We could have whiz-banged around the galaxy.' I sighed.

'I wonder what's happening at home,' said Max. 'They must be out of their minds with worry. Mum and Dad anyway. My sister must be out of her mind with happiness. She's probably thrown a party.'

I grinned. The radio was turned off. I knew that my parents would still beep and squeak at me, and I needed to concentrate. The Zordethian sun was far behind us and we were racing past squillions of stars that filled the space window with light.

'According to the time and space charts I've looked at, you could be home before you're missed. We're going into gigadrive soon and it will send us back in time. Don't ask me to explain how because I don't know.'

Max pointed to a fiery comet that streaked past his window, leaving showers of tiny bright lights.

'I'm going to be an astronaut when I grow up,' he told me. 'A real spaceman. I'll find a way to come back and see you.'

I felt a strange kind of stress lump coming up on my forehead. It was just a little one. Now, according to those space charts, and the speed I was travelling, I should have been pulling the lever about ... now.

Both Max and I were thrown back into our seats.

'What on Earth ... '

'What on Zordeth ... '

The stars had gone now. Instead we were moving through a spiralling tunnel at enormous speed.

There were noises coming from inside the giga-drive control.

'I hope it holds,' I muttered.

The tunnel widened. And widened again. Our speed seemed to increase, then suddenly everything changed. There was just blackness.

'Do you know where we are?' Max asked.

'Sort of,' I said, but I was as panicky as a pinchpod at a party because I didn't have a clue where we were. There were no stars around at all. Nothing. Just empty darkness.

Then suddenly I saw a few bright pinpoints of light. We'd come through the other side. We'd made it somewhere, I just didn't know where.

I turned on my space radio. There was a lot of muffled noise. I adjusted it. Suddenly Max had jumped out of his cloud seat and was spinning around like a fitzywheel.

'Music! Earth music.'

Well, it didn't sound like music to me. It sounded like the worst habble gabble I'd ever heard. I directed the ship towards the sounds, and slowly but surely they got louder. I studied Dad's space charts carefully.

Max, meantime, was doing some kind of weird native dance and saying, 'That's rock and roll.' Was he hungry then? But he didn't eat rocks, did he? Maybe he'd like to try one of Mum's krystalumps after all. I hoped it wouldn't upset his stomachs.

I reached into my pocket, pulled out a big one and handed it to him.

Max looked at the krystalump and cautiously nibbled at it.

'This is a rock,' he said.

'Mum made it,' I told him. 'You said something about rock and roll. I'm not sure about the roll part but you might like to try our rock.'

Max said, 'Um, ah, thanks very much, but I might wait until I get home.' He put the krystalump in his pocket.

Oh well, I'd tried. I switched on the visual monitor and flicked from screen to screen. Great bells of banglee! I saw strange aliens in weird clothing. I saw water and an alien standing on what looked like a lava sledge being towed by a small craft. How odd! Then there were tall buildings. And what was that? Big aliens feeding small aliens and helping them hold cups. I saw long tubes of aliens curling through strange countryside. And white-topped mountains.

Max was waving his long arms, pointing and laughing.

I kept the craft on course. We passed one medium-sized sun, then two small planets, one covered in cloud. All that horrible noise was coming from

... let's see, that planet there – the third from the sun. The one that was circled by one silver moon.

I asked Max a lot of questions – about his life, about school, about his family and friends. There suddenly seemed so little time left.

The planet, the one Max called Earth, swirled in front of us. I cautiously dipped the spaceship down through the darkness of space, through the soft white clouds, through ...

We were high above Earth in a blue sky above huge oceans. Now I had to study those charts that Dad had made. If I flicked the lever this way, and moved that way ...

Max just couldn't keep still. He jumped up and down in his cloud seat. I guessed he was happy to be home. That was okay. I'd feel the same way. It was just that ... I don't know. My forehead was starting to ache.

I tried to keep the spaceship well out of sight but it wasn't really possible. We passed a strange hopper with whirling blades on top of it. It suddenly started to spin round and round.

'What's it doing?' I asked Max.

'The pilot's going nuts,' said Max. 'He's just seen his first UFO. You'd better land soon or they'll send the air force out after you.'

I had no idea what the air force was but I definitely didn't want to be forced to air anything. Let's see where we were. If I moved the ship around this way. Whoops! Nearly hit that small flying machine. If I headed for that strip of strange green grass with those wavy trees, if I could just get this ship to land behind one ...

I pushed the button that released the metal prods from the bottom of the spaceship, and we landed nicely just behind a clump of Earth trees.

When we'd touched down, the first thing I noticed was the habble gabble coming from outside the ship.

'What's that?'

'Birds,' said Max. 'Good old Earth birds.'

I didn't know that word. I stood up, stretched, then opened the side panel. Max pushed past me and hopped out. 'I know where I am! This is the park near where I live.'

I climbed out too. We stood underneath big furry-looking trees. Strange, winged creatures flew around. The sun was large and hot. Suddenly I didn't know what to say to Max. I heard more habble gabble coming from behind the trees.

'You'd better go,' said Max. 'Lots of people use this park. If they find you here, they'll, they'll ... '

'They'll probably put me in some kind of zoo,' I clicked sadly. 'I'm really sorry about what happened, Max.'

'You've been great. No one's ever going to believe this,' said Max. 'I'll always remember you.'

I reached deep into my pocket. Deep down. If I was lucky ... I pulled out a small bubble packet. 'I don't know if these will grow on Earth but if they do you can make a squillion out of them. They're space-flower seeds. You sing to them and they sing back.'

'That sounds cool,' said Max.

'No, they're not cool. They need a lot of sunlight and they're very emotional. I reckon they're ... what's the Earth word ... daggy.'

There was a stress lump the size of a dorpo on my forehead. It was just that we never did get a chance to say half the things we wanted to. And we could have been friends. Great friends. Fiddling folly-foops, it just wasn't fair.

Max came over to me. He jumped on my shoes. The weight nearly killed me but I managed to smile. I jumped on his. Then I climbed back into my spaceship, just in time. Three alien children had just walked up to Max. They were staring up at me through the space window. Max was saying something and they were shaking their heads. One was running towards the ship. Max was running after him.

If I couldn't lift the ship off the ground I'd be as stranded as a cuddy in a coody. I pulled a lever, pressed a button, and there was a sound like the engine was being strangled.

The spacecraft started to twitch, then shudder. There were creaking noises coming from the gigadrive. I looked out the window. Max was holding onto an alien boy. I could tell he was worried. I was worried.

Then suddenly, with a shake, the ship lifted off. It hovered above the ground for a hecta-second or two then it whiz-banged up into the white clouds. It paused, gave another shake, then made a final leap into space.

I was up there, above Max's planet – the noisy one, third from their sun. I'd remember. Max would remember.

I sighed, then studied my space charts. There were a few shivers and trembles when I went into gigadrive, and my hearts missed a few beats. The tunnel seemed to go on forever, but, just when I thought I might be stranded, I was out of it. The sky slowly filled up with familiar stars.

I plotted my course for home. I'd sort things out with Mum and Dad. Soon Gike and I would be able to jet all over the galaxy together chewing gubble-bum. Everything would go back to normal, yet nothing felt the same.

Max wouldn't be there.

I guessed there was only one thing to do. I'd just have to go back to Earth one day.

Yes, that's what I'd do. But meantime I'd settle for a few of Mum's krystalumps.

ABOUT THE
AUTHOR

MOYA SIMONS lives in Sydney and has two grown-up daughters, Suzy and Tamie. Moya spends a lot of time writing and says that marshmallows and chocolate help to inspire her. She has many pot-plants and admits to occasionally singing to them, insisting that when they're in a good mood they will flap their leaves and sing back.

Moya's other books are *Iggy From Outer Space*, *Sit Down, Mum, There's Something I've Got to Tell You*, *Dead Meat!*, *Dead Average!*, *Dead Worried!* and *Fourteen Something*. Her books have also been published in England and the USA.

Moya loves watching 'Star Trek' on TV, reads a lot of science fiction and is determined to come back in her next life as an astronaut. She especially enjoyed writing *Spacenapped!* because most science fiction stories are about what happens to aliens 'down here'. *Spacenapped!* is about what actually goes on 'up there'.

ABOUT THE
ILLUSTRATOR

LEIGH HOBBS was born in Melbourne but grew up in Bairnsdale in country Victoria. After leaving art school, Leigh created Larry and Lizzy, two huge caricature sculptures for Sydney's Luna Park, now at the Powerhouse Museum.

Many of Leigh's cartoons have appeared in the *Age*, and he has illustrated many children's books including *Mr Knuckles*, *Belly Busters*, and *Around the World With Miss Smith and Miss Jones*.

Although allergic to cats, Leigh is arguably most famous for his *Old Tom* series, featuring the adventures of a chubby, flea-ridden, but lovable puss of the same name.